My Teacher
Is An Idiom

My Teacher Is An Idiom

by Jamie Gilson
Illustrations by Paul Meisel

Clarion Books
Houghton Mifflin Harcourt
Boston   New York

Clarion Books

215 Park Avenue South

New York, New York 10003

Copyright © 2015 by Jamie Gilson

Illustrations copyright © 2015 by Paul Meisel

Clarion Books is an imprint of

Houghton Mifflin Harcourt Publishing Company.

www.hmhco.com

The text was set in Garamond 3 LT Std.

Library of Congress Cataloging-in-Publication Data

Gilson, Jamie.

My teacher is an idiom / Jamie Gilson ; illustrations by Paul Meisel.

pages cm

Summary: Second-grader Richard finds himself in big trouble during
Mind Your Manners Month when he unwittingly captures the attention of
Patrick, the class clown, and Sophie, a French girl who has trouble with idioms.

ISBN 978-0-544-05680-0 (hardback)

[1. Etiquette—Fiction. 2. Schools—Fiction. 3. English language—
Idioms—Fiction. 4. Behavior—Fiction. 5. Humorous stories.] I. Title.

PZ7.G4385My 2015

[Fic]—dc23

2014027798

Manufactured in the United States of America

DOC 10 9 8 7 6 5 4 3 2 1

4500545129

Contents

To Henry Hutter Gilson, Samurai Scribe

— 1 —
You'll Laugh Your Head Off

The banner in the lunchroom said MIND YOUR MANNERS! It was new. And red. You couldn't miss it. A bunch of third graders painted it. They got caught spitting watermelon seeds and cherry pits. The watermelon seeds won.

I wasn't spitting seeds or pits. I was just hanging out. Kids were leaving the lunchroom for the playground, and I hadn't even started to eat.

I stared at my lunch. That's when Patrick tapped me on the shoulder. "Hey, Richie," he went.

He plopped himself down in the chair next to

me and said, "Richie, this is your lucky day. You wanna know why I'm still here? I'm gonna sit with you today while you eat, that's why. Mind your manners, right?" He pointed up at the banner. "And—"

"Wait a minute," I interrupted him. Patrick likes jokes. He likes to play jokes on you, and he likes to tell jokes. Sometimes he's funny. Mostly he's not.

He didn't sit down to eat with me. He wanted to tell me a joke. Here's how I knew. He had a dollar bill taped to each of his ears, that's how. People don't usually wear money.

"Wait a minute," I said. "Why are you calling me Richie? My name is Richard. Nobody calls me Richie. Not even my mom."

"I can, because we're friends," he said.

Friends? Just the day before, I lost two front teeth because of Patrick. *Two!* Top ones. He knew they were loose, too. Every kid in Mrs. Zookey's class knew. All week long I'd been showing the kids at Table Two how they wiggled. I even showed them how one was looser than the other, so they'd for sure come out at different times.

He knew it, all right. And that's why he gave me this big fat gummy octopus at recess. It was licorice. I like licorice, but it was a bad idea to bite it. *Now* I know. But at that minute, I was just super hungry.

I took a bite.

I bit. But I didn't swallow. That's because my two front teeth weren't loose anymore. They were stuck in the octopus. They were not stuck in me.

"Eeewww, gross!" Patrick yelled, and he ran around pulling kids over to see me and my teeth. He was going, *"Eeewwww!* Everybody look. Everybody look at Richie!"

My chin was bloody.

In my hand I had a licorice octopus with two teeth sticking out of it.

"Eeewwww, gross!" said the kids on the playground. *"Eeewwww!"*

That's the kind of friend Patrick is.

Patrick is trouble. What's more, he gets *me* in trouble, too. I decided right then, right there, on the playground, that I would never let Patrick get me in trouble again. "I'll get you back, Patrick," I told him. "Just you wait and see."

By now Patrick and me were just about the only ones left in the lunchroom. I had a tuna salad sandwich sitting in front of me. I hadn't touched it. I couldn't figure out how to eat it with two missing teeth.

It smelled so good. I tore off a piece of it with my side teeth. It made a ginormous mess. Goopy tuna salad oozed onto my fingers.

Patrick laughed. So I stuck out my tongue at him. And I started making a plan to get him back. It was his fault.

He smiled at me like nothing was wrong. Then he wiggled his head to make the dollar bills flap.

"Everybody else has gone outside to play four-square and kickball," Patrick told me, "but I'm still here to cheer you up."

No way, I thought. I licked the tuna salad off my fingers. It was good, but it didn't fill me up.

Patrick shook his head again, and the dollar bills shivered. "You look super sad with those two teeth gone," he went on. "So, I'm here to tell you a joke that will make you laugh your head off. You won't be able to figure it out. I'll be here to help you out. Okay?"

Not okay. I knew what he wanted. It was as clear as the nose on his face. He wanted me to say, "Patrick, why do you have dollar bills taped to your ears?" so he could tell me the joke.

I didn't say it.

I didn't say it because I already knew that joke. My mom told it to me the day she got her ears pierced. I laughed my head off when she told it. I did that because it was polite and my mom is big on polite. Also I really thought it was funny.

This time, I would get Patrick. "No, no!" I told him. "Me first! Remember, I'm the one without the teeth." I gave him a sad, toothless smile and stuck out my hand to stop him from talking.

"It hurt a whole lot when you pulled my teeth out, but now I'm okay," I said. "Maybe I can cheer *you* up. You must feel really bad that it was your fault. I've got a good joke, too. This one is so funny, you'll break up! I'll have to sweep you off the floor."

The thing is, I could tell just by the dollar bills swinging from his ears that Patrick's joke was the exact same joke as the one my mom told me. I had to tell it fast. I had to tell it first.

"So," I said quick, "here it is. Ready, set, go! Do you know what a pirate charges to pierce your ears?"

His mouth dropped open. He knew the answer. He knew it because that's what he was about to ask *me.* But now it was *my* joke.

"You know what 'pierce' is?" I asked him. "It's when you poke a needle in somebody's ear so they can stick an earring in the hole."

He nodded and the dollars moved. "Basketball players have them," he said. "And rock stars. But I—"

"Okay, ready?" I went on, talking faster. "Okay, I'll tell the joke again. How much does a pirate charge to pierce your ears? Take your time," I said. "Ask a friend." I was stringing him along.

I looked around the lunchroom and spotted this girl from our room sitting a couple of tables over. This was only her second day at Sumac School. Our teacher, Mrs. Zookey, had told us to be especially nice to her because she mostly spoke this other language. The language was French. Mrs. Zookey said the kid had studied English in school. It was a subject, like math. Chances are she wasn't good at pirate jokes.

"I think the new girl won't help you a lot," I told him. "Sorry about that."

Patrick opened his mouth. I think he started to give me the answer, but I said it first, loud and clear. "A dollar bill is also called a buck. And that's what a pirate charges to pierce your ears. You've got two ears. He charges a buck an ear. A pirate is a *buccaneer*. It sounds the same as 'buck an ear.' Get it?"

Patrick got it. He had a buck hanging on each ear. He got it, but I said it. I won! Yay, me!

He pulled the dollar bills off his ears and stuffed them in his pocket. "Not funny," he said, and he crossed his arms. "You wouldn't have gotten mine. It was much, much better. But I'm not gonna tell it to you, so now you'll never know."

I smiled at him. Then I opened my sandwich like it was a book. Carefully, slowly, I peeled off two fingers full of tuna salad. I ate it like it was a batch of cookie dough I'd scooped from the bottom of a bowl. Yum. I licked my fingers clean. I was happy.

Patrick looked up at the sign. "Richie," he said, "you've gotta have the worst table manners in the whole world."

— 2 —
The Mosquito

Patrick had brought sushi for his lunch. It was gone. He'd already eaten it. He still had his dessert, though. It was big purple grapes. I watched him pick them off the stem, one by one. He tossed them up high in the air and caught them on his tongue. Actually, he caught four of them. He missed three. They bounced on the floor.

"So that's the world's *best* table manners?" I asked him.

"Tossing and catching grapes on your tongue takes skill," he said. "You gotta practice. Also, it is nice and clean. Licking food off your fingers is disgusting. It gives you big fat germs, like for sore throats and flu. It is also bad manners. Ask anybody." He stood up and stomped on the grapes that had hit the floor. "Pow!" he went. "Pow! Pow!"

Then he asked, "You got any dessert?"

I held up this plastic bowl of raspberry Jell-O. Mom packed it with two ice cubes, but it was in my locker all morning, so it was ooshy. I pinched it to see just how ooshy it was, then I peeled off the lid.

I took out my spoon. It was green plastic with a frog at the top. I took it home every day after school, washed it, and brought it back the next day. My mom and me, we're into green.

"Go on outside. Don't worry about me," I told Patrick. "I'll be there in a couple of minutes. I just want to eat my dessert."

Patrick stared at my red Jell-O. He smiled.

"No, no, no," he said. "Friends are supposed to

keep you company. I'm not mad about the joke. I'll stay." His smile got bigger.

"Besides," he went on, "I just got this great idea. You're gonna love it. When I did this at home, my dad laughed his head off. He said I'm so funny that someday I'll get my own TV talk show and make tons of money. I'll tell you how I broke him up so you can do it, too, okay?" He handed me a straw. "Here, use this," he said.

"No, thank you," I told him, minding my manners. "I finished my milk." I didn't want milk shooting out of my nose.

"Oh, it's not for milk," he said. "It's for your dessert. That stuff's way too mushy for a spoon. You'd get it all over you. Use the straw. Okay, I'll show you how. It's a great way to eat. It's even got a name."

The Jell-O was ooshy. That was true. Sometimes Patrick knows what he's talking about. He isn't *always* trouble. I took the straw. It was white with red stripes.

There's a box of plain straws in the lunchroom over by the milk cartons, but every day Patrick brings his own. Patrick's straws are fat, like the kind you get with a smoothie. I've seen him shoot little wads of paper through them. Once he zapped a kid's neck and she never knew what hit her. She swatted the spot like she'd been bit by a fly.

I looked through the straw he'd handed me. I had to be sure it didn't have a paper wad inside. Or a worm. Or maybe even a wet booger. I wasn't about to let him fool me.

It was empty.

Patrick really was mad at me for telling his joke first. Now he was treating me like a baby, like I didn't know what the special word for drinking through a straw is.

"It's called sucking," I told him.

"No, no. This way is very, very special," he said. "The real name for this is The Mosquito."

"Mosquito?" I asked.

"*The* Mosquito," he answered. "See, you suck the ooshy red stuff up through the straw like a lady mosquito sucks blood. For one thing, it tastes better, and for another thing, it's way better manners than dripping ooshy red stuff all over yourself.

"Yum," he said. He licked his lips. Then he looked at me and waited.

"Okay, I told you how," he said. "So now you can do it."

"I don't think so," I told him. "I'll just use my spoon. Besides, you didn't see it, but Mr. E. just came in, and I bet he'd say that eating like a mosquito sucks blood is gross."

Patrick turned to look. "Come on, Mr. E. won't kill you," he said. "Cross my heart and hope to die."

Mr. E. doesn't kill kids, but you don't want to mess with him. He is vice principal of Sumac School. His real name is Mr. Economopoulos, but he lets us call him Mr. E. He always wears a green Sumac School T-shirt. There's a stack of them in his office. My mom said the PTA ordered them special, in his size, XXXXL. One thing Mr. E. does is he keeps his eyes peeled for bad stuff. When he sees it, look out.

I checked. Mr. E. did not have either of his eyes on us. He was using them both to look out the window. He was watching kids on the playground. It had rained in the night, and there were puddles, perfect for stomping in. He was on the lookout. Some kids say he has eyes in the back of his head, too. Maybe so.

The lunchroom monitors were at the other end of the cafeteria. They're moms who sign up for lunch duty. They wear nets on their hair. They serve soup for kids who buy lunch, and microwave stuff that kids bring from home. When the line closes, they mostly just talk to each other. They'd shoo us out soon.

"Go ahead," Patrick said. "Trust me. Just do it."

I don't have to do what Patrick says. I put the red and white straw down and picked up my green spoon.

He shrugged. "Fine. Don't do it. It would have been fun. You know, Richie, you don't have near enough fun." He shook his head.

Okay, I thought, maybe he was right. What could go wrong sucking Jell-O up a straw?

So I picked up the straw. I stuck it deep down into the cup. The straw leaned to the side. I sucked on it till the straw had maybe an inch of the red raspberry stuff inside. Then I turned the straw over and sucked the stuff out. "Eating like that would take forever," I told him. I grabbed my spoon again.

Mr. E. turned around and nodded to us. Patrick sat up very straight and smiled like someone had said "Cheese!"

He thought he had Mr. E. wrapped around his little finger.

— 3 —

Slurrp!

"Mr. E.! Mr. E.!" Patrick called. If you say it just right, "Mr. E." sounds like "mystery," and that's the way Patrick said it. "Mr. E.," he went on, "I think I've got a quarter stuck behind my ear. Would you look?"

Mr. E. does magic. He's good at it. I think he likes showing off. He smiled and walked over to us. He stared in Patrick's ear. "I see wax," he said. "I even see patches of what appear to be sand dunes, but I see no quarter."

Two tables over, the new kid from France was watching.

Mr. E. showed us his hands. They were totally empty. Then he reached over and pulled a coin from behind Patrick's ear. "No quarter there," he said. "Just a penny." He held it up. "But I saved it from your sand dunes."

We laughed. I mean, sand dunes in your ears?

"You know the rules," Mr. E. said. "Twenty minutes for lunch, and then thirty minutes of quality exercise on the playground. The two of you should be outside right now. I'll give you a penny for your thoughts on that, Richard." He held it out.

I took the penny and put it in my jeans pocket. "I'm thinking I miss my teeth," I said, and I showed him the empty space.

He smiled and shook his head. "Hard to bite without incisors," he said. "Sorry I can't conjure up any of those. It's nice of you to stay with him, Patrick. But still, hurry it up." He looked at his watch. "I'll give you five more minutes."

On his way out to the playground, he stopped and talked to the new kid. She started putting on her jacket. Yesterday, Mrs. Zookey told Dawn Marie to sit with the new kid at lunch. They both sit at Table

Two with Patrick and me. Today, Dawn Marie must have gone outside.

For sure Dawn Marie was out jumping rope with this bunch of girls. When they jump, they sing princess stuff like "Cinderella dressed in yella" and "Sleeping Beauty caught a cootie."

Patrick waited until the outside door shut behind Mr. E. Then he said, "You've still got four minutes, at least. I saw a kid push another kid down in the mud. Mr. E. will be gone for a while.

"The thing is, you were doing it all wrong. Here's how The Mosquito works."

He pulled another straw out of his lunchbox. This one had blue stripes. Then he reached for my dessert.

"If you're gonna do it right," he said, "you gotta warm up. Like this." He stuck the empty straw in his mouth, pointed it straight out, and took in a huge breath.

Then he let it out slow through the straw. He put the straw next to a stray grape on the table. He blew twice until the grape was right at the edge. Then he sucked in and caught the grape, just when it was about to fall. He took the straw out of his mouth, and the grape bounced on the floor.

"I've got very, very good lungs," he said. "You want to try?"

"Not really," I told him. "I know how to breathe in and out. I do it all the time."

"Okay by me," he said, "but now watch *this*." He stood up with the straw with blue stripes in his mouth, stuck it in my Jell-O cup, and sucked in. Way in. He did a ginormous vacuum-cleaner thing.

SLURRP!

Boy, did he suck up my dessert. It sounded like a hog snarfing. I've never actually heard a hog, but I bet it sounds just like that. Patrick's mouth was full. He took the straw out and let some of the red stuff drool over his bottom lip.

Red raspberry drops rolled slowly down his chin. One by one, they plopped on the table. I knew this was bigtime bad table manners, but it broke me up. Patrick's dad was right. The Mosquito was good enough to go viral on YouTube. I was just about to crack up, totally, when the new kid rushed over.

"It is blood? He is sick?" she asked. She wasn't laughing. She was scared.

Mrs. Zookey told us to talk slow to the new kid so she could understand.

"Hi, Sophie," I said. Mrs. Zookey had written her name on the board. Sophie told the class she was from a town called Rennes. Mrs. Zookey wrote that down, too. Nobody had been there, not even Patrick.

Sophie looked like a regular person. She had this long brown hair and she was wearing glasses with cool red rims. I tried being friendly, and I talked loud so she could understand. "HOW ARE YOU?" I yelled.

"HE IS SICK?" she yelled back, pointing at Patrick.

Patrick puffed out his cheeks. He looked like he might throw up. Then he opened his mouth. Red stuff oozed over his teeth. "I, Dracula," he said. Sort of. *I* understood him. I'm not sure Sophie did. She was staring at the red rivers running down his chin. They were dripping into a gory puddle on the table.

She put her hand over her mouth, like if she didn't, she might scream. Or lose her lunch. Whichever came first.

Patrick stuck out his tongue. He'd oozed out most of what he'd sucked in, but a little lake of it still floated on his tongue. It looked funny, but I thought a whole big ocean would be even funnier.

So while Sophie still had her eye on Patrick, I grabbed my green frog spoon. I scooped it full of squishy red stuff. I dumped that on my tongue. I did it two times. Then I tugged the sleeve of her coat so she'd look at me instead of Patrick.

When she did, her eyes got even wider. I crossed mine, and tried to say, "I, vampire bat." This is very hard to do with your tongue piled with oosh. It came out, "I, an-ire at."

I flapped my elbows. I was Number-One Super-Awesome An-ire At. Patrick closed his mouth to laugh at my bat. When he did, red stuff oozed out his nose.

Sophie leaned over to look closer. She frowned. "You do not need help?" she asked, like maybe she should call 911. She thought it was real blood! This was so much fun.

Patrick swallowed. "Watch this," he told her, waving his arms so she'd be sure to look at him. "I'll show you how my *real* vampire gets Richie's wimpy bat."

He stuck the blue striped straw back in his mouth and sucked up the rest of the red Jell-O. When the straw was full of red stuff, he pointed it straight at me! Then he pointed it at Sophie. Back and forth. Back and forth. This was not funny. He was going to squirt red oosh at me and the new kid, too.

If my mouth hadn't been so full, I'd have yelled at him. But I didn't need to. Sophie was already doing it. *"No!"* she yelled, and backed away from him. *"No!"* She had a super-loud voice.

"Stop!" She stepped on one of the grapes that Patrick had stomped on, slipped, and fell *splat* on her bottom. I couldn't help her. I couldn't even talk.

I tried to swallow. I really did, but instead I took a weird breath. My nose began to tickle, bad. I tried to sniff up the tickle. I tucked my head down and pressed hard on my mouth. I tried to hold it in. I tried, but I couldn't. I couldn't swallow, either. What I had to do was sneeze.

"Aahhh . . . ahhhh . . ." I went. I closed my eyes tight. I lifted my head.

"I'm outta here!" Patrick yelled.

"AH-AH-AH-CHOOOOOOO!"

I know you're supposed to cover up sneezes. My mom says it's polite and also keeps people from getting your germs. I know it, no kidding, but I didn't want that icky stuff all over my hands. It would have been disgusting. Also, I didn't want to get red mush on the honeybee shirt I'd gotten for Endangered Animal Day. I'd only worn it, like, three times.

So I sneezed straight out. I could feel the fake vampire blood spray out of my mouth and my nose—way out.

But guess who was back in the cafeteria? Guess

who heard Sophie's *"No! No!"* when he got back? Guess who rushed right up to our table?

Okay, now guess whose green XXXXL-size Sumac School T-shirt had big red blobs all over it? Guess whose shirt looked like he'd just had a giant bloody nose?

I didn't have to guess. I knew.

— 4 —

Hide!

I couldn't hide under the table. It was too late. Mr. E. was standing right in front of me. I didn't need to give him a penny for his thoughts, either.

He looked down at his shirt. His face was almost as red as the goop. He looked straight at me. "You," he said, very quiet. *"You!"* he said, a lot louder.

What was he going to say? *You* will eat in a closet from now on, the one with the mops and the buckets? *You* will leave school right now forever and ever? *You* . . . what? I knew for sure *who* he meant by *You*. It wasn't Patrick. Patrick hadn't sneezed. He had swallowed. And he must have had a napkin. He got the red stuff off his nose, at least.

"I . . . I . . . I . . ." I began. If I said it wasn't my fault, Mr. E. would never believe me. He watched it happen.

He waited.

I waited, too. I tried to think. If I said Patrick started it, that might make things worse.

The lunchroom moms were heading toward us, but Mr. E. waved them back.

"I . . . I . . . I'm sorry," I told him finally.

"You . . ." He reached in his pocket and handed me a pack of tissues. "You need to blow your nose." The stuff I blew out was gross.

Sophie had scrambled to her feet. "You . . ." she said, pointing at me, "are stupid."

I sucked in my breath. So did Patrick. Actually, so did Mr. E. That didn't stop Sophie.

"You," she said, pointing at Patrick, "are also stu—"

I cut her off. "You can't say that," I told her. "That's like . . . swearing."

"You just started to call me a *name*," Patrick told her. "I think that's against school law. Mr. E. will have to call your mother or father or caregiver. Right, Mr. E.?"

Sophie didn't look scared anymore. She shook her hair, put her hands on her hips, and narrowed her eyes. "I do not call your name," she told Patrick. "I do not know it, but I know you are stu—"

"Hold on," Mr. E. said. "Let's take this talk back to my office. I've got to change my shirt. The kids from the playground would freak out if they saw it. All three of you, pack up and move. On the double!"

I was in trouble again, and I knew why. Patrick.

We gathered our stuff, and Mr. E. marched us down the hall.

When we got to his office, he pointed at three chairs across from his desk. We sat in them. "I don't have much time," Mr. E. said, "so let's get right to the bottom of this." Then he tortured us.

He didn't turn into a werewolf and drool. He didn't roar. He didn't even call our mothers, fathers, or caregivers. He talked about manners. Manners!

"We have a big problem here," he said. "As you know, this is Mind Your Manners Month here at Sumac School. And it's clear to me that you two boys don't understand good manners, especially good lunchroom manners."

He turned to me and said, "Richard, you should always, always cover your mouth when you sneeze. Especially if your mouth is full of food."

"Yes, Mr. E.," I said.

"Richard will be sure to remember that," Patrick said. This was true, but Patrick didn't need to rub it in. He quick-wiped a mess of sticky red stuff off his chin and onto his sleeve.

Then Mr. E. talked to all three of us about being nice. Nice! "That's what manners are all about," he said. He made us say nice things to each other. This was not easy.

Patrick told Sophie he'd heard on the History Channel that France gave us the Statue of Liberty, and he thought that was nice.

I told Sophie that we were very glad she had moved to our town and our school and that we were very happy she was sitting with us at Table Two in Mrs. Zookey's room. I told her I was sure that very soon we would all be friends. She didn't believe me. I could tell.

Sophie said she couldn't think of anything nice to say. She said that was because we were not nice. She said she thought we were stupid.

This time Mr. E. cut her off. "Why do you use such a strong word about these boys?" he asked her.

"I call a cat a cat," Sophie said.

"You can't call me a cat. What's that supposed to mean?" Patrick asked her.

"We say it in France," she said. "But we say it in French. It means I call things what they *are,* and you are—"

Patrick told Sophie he thought she just didn't understand that in our school we didn't call people bad names. She rolled her eyes at him.

"You speak English well, Sophie," Mr. E. said, talking slow because she was new. "Do you understand all my words?"

She nodded. "I know American words," she said. "I learn them at my school in France. Also, I learn at the restaurant of my papa."

"Ah, yes, of course. When I talked with your father yesterday, he told me he is a chef. His restaurant just opened?"

Sophie nodded. "It is called Chez Paul Henri, the name of my papa. In English you would say 'The House of Paul Henri.' His specialty, it is the *escargots*."

"That's splendid," Mr. E. told her. "I like snails very much."

Snails? That word meant *snails?* Sophie's father

cooked real snails? Mr. E. ate them? I started to ask if this was true, but Mr. E. kept talking.

"Sophie," he said, "you seem like a cheerful girl. Tell me, what did these boys do to make you so angry?"

She smiled a little smile. *This is it,* I thought. *She's going to give us away.* She was even right. The Mosquito turned out to be really stupid. Patrick closed his eyes.

Sophie shook her head. "I am making the white cabbage," she said.

"Wait up." Mr. E. leaned forward. Red goop from his shirt smeared on his desk, but he didn't even notice. "I'm afraid we've got our wires crossed," he told her. "You say you are cooking white cabbage?"

"*Making* white cabbage," Sophie said. "We say that in France."

"Only you say it in French," I said.

"Oui." She nodded. "People say it. My papa, he say it. It is not real cabbage like he cooks. It means," she went on, "'In my head I do not think of . . . anything.'"

"You're drawing a blank," I said.

She blinked. "A blank? I think so," she said. "I remember nothings."

"Or maybe," Patrick said, "the cat's got your tongue."

Sophie frowned. "No. I have no cat," she said. "I have the dog. His name is called Milou. Milou will not bite my tongue, even if I stick it out." She stuck out her tongue. Then she shrugged. "But naturally he is not here."

I looked at Patrick, and Patrick looked at me. We both shook our heads. Maybe it was different in France.

Mr. E. slapped his hand on his forehead. "I see. The problem here is idioms. You're using an *idiom* to explain that you don't know what happened. A

French idiom. Every language has them. Do you boys know what an idiom is?"

I must have been making white cabbage, too. *Idiom* didn't mean anything to me. Patrick said, "Huh?" It was like he didn't know *idiom* and didn't want to meet it.

"It's good to know about idioms. You use them all the time," Mr. E. went on. He was all excited. He leaned over and got even more bat blood on his desk. "An idiom is a group of words that don't mean what they say. It's like when you tell someone, 'It's raining cats and dogs.' You don't mean there are wet kittens and puppies falling out of the sky. You're just saying it's raining very hard, or . . . Can you think of another idiom, Richard?"

I shook my head and shifted around in the chair. I mean, I just use regular words.

"How about you, Sophie?" he asked her. "Do you understand what we're talking about?"

She smiled. "I know my idiom," she told him. "We say, *Il pleut des cordes.* 'It rains ropes.' We do not say dogs and cats fall off the sky. They do not."

"Ropes of rain," Mr. E. said. "That's good. If there was a windy shower, you'd be all tied up in water knots."

Patrick kept it going. "I ate a bite of cabbage once," he said. "I don't know if it was white. It was

Saint Patrick's Day, so maybe it was green." He looked at Mr. E. and smiled way too big. "It was very tasty."

Sophie stared at us. She knew what had happened in the lunchroom. But she didn't tell. She could have. She could have told Mr. E. she knew my mouth was full on purpose to gross her out. But she didn't. She could have said Patrick was just about to squirt us both with a straw full of fake blood. But she didn't. She also didn't say she was sorry she called us stupid.

"*Stupid* is a good word, no?" she asked Mr. E.

"It is not," Mr. E. told her. "It's a mean way of saying someone is not very smart. These boys are smart, but they don't always do what they should. You may have meant they have bad manners. That is certainly true. I've seen much too much of it lately. Especially in the lunchroom. I've heard way too much loud burping."

He looked straight at Patrick. "It's clear," he said, "that Mind Your Manners Month is not enough."

Then he looked at me. "There will be consequences for what you did, Richard. Do you know what consequences are?"

"Yes, sir," I said. "It means something is going to happen that I won't like."

"That," he told me, "is exactly what it means. Something will happen because of what you did. I'll be in touch with Mrs. Zookey.

"Now, back to your room!" he told the three of us. "Lunchtime is almost over, and I still have to change this shirt." I saw a pile of new ones stacked on a shelf. It'd be a quick change.

His face was grim. "Don't run," he told us, "but step on it."

— 5 —

Consequences

As soon as we were far enough away, I took a deep breath. "'There will be consequences,'" I said.

"Don't sweat it," Patrick said. "We got off with bad manners. Bad manners is nothing. Bad manners is like eating spaghetti with your fingers. I never do that. It would be piggy."

"Mr. E. said big burps were bad," I told him.

"I heard that. What was he thinking? I'm really good at those. *Urp!*" He let off a huge one just to show us. Really, it was huge. "See, if I did that in China, it would be good, my father says. He says it would be like going 'I liked my food a lot.'" Patrick burped again, even louder.

"You are not in China," Sophie said to him. "You are here. I think it is not the same here." Then she asked me, "Do I have the consequences, too? I do not know this word."

"You don't have to do anything," I told her. "We got away with it. We fooled Mr. E. for sure. And you helped. You didn't tell."

She shook her head and hurried on to the water fountain.

When we caught up to her, she asked, "Mr. Economopoulos, he is the important person, no?"

"Mr. E. is very, very important," Patrick told her. "He is vice principal. He is scarier than the principal. Mr. E. is the Big Cheese." Patrick lowered his voice. "We call him Mystery. You know, like one of those scary stories you can't figure out." He grinned at me. "You want to know why we call him Mystery?

Did you see him take the penny from behind my ear in the lunchroom?"

"I see it," she said.

"Mystery!" Patrick said. "See, he does things you can't figure out, magical things. He's a magician, you know? Maybe he's even a real wizard, like at Hogwarts. I bet you heard him say he was going to change his shirt. He *will* make it change, too. Next time you see him, you'll see the same green shirt, but those red spots will be totally gone. All he's got to do is wave a wand or maybe say a magic word like *abracadabra!*" He waved his arms. "The spots will go away. Totally."

"He makes things appear, too. Like the penny," I told her. Patrick and I were both fooling this kid. It was easy.

"He does not scare me," Sophie said. "I like him. When I meet him, he tells me his family is from Greece. He comes here when he is young, like I do.

Then his father has a restaurant, like mine does now."

"Okay," I said, "but remember that he's the Big Cheese, and at this school the Big Cheese doesn't like it when you call somebody stupid."

"What you do before in the lunchroom is called bad manners?" she asked.

"Right," Patrick said. "No big deal. You heard what Mr. E. said. Richard shouldn't sneeze with his mouth open."

"But," she said, "you were both —"

Brrrring. The bell in the hall rang. Lunch period was over.

"It was a mess of bad manners," I told her. "That's all."

When I opened the door to our room, Mrs. Zookey was talking on her cell phone. She was at her desk, sitting on her chair. It was a big blue exercise ball. Her silvery cat earrings were bobbing up

and down as she bounced. Her red hair was bounc-
ing, too.

She looked up, and I could tell she was not happy.
She was shaking her head, and she was not smiling.
Just like he said he would, Mr. E. had called her.

Dawn Marie, the other Table Two kid, watched us. She knew something was up. She'd left the new kid behind in the lunchroom. She went out to the playground to sing songs and jump rope. The new kid got in trouble. This was not good.

"You okay?" she asked Sophie when she sat down.

"No, thank you," Sophie told her. I think she was trying to be polite.

My friend Ben wasn't at Table Two anymore. Mrs. Zookey had moved him to Table Three. She said we talked too much. This was not fair. He is my best friend. At Table Three, Ben sits next to Aiden. They were talking.

Most of the kids in the room weren't paying any attention to us. They were staring at the ceiling. That's because it looked weird. Mrs. Zookey must have spent the whole lunch hour turning our room into a rainforest. She did this because in social studies we were learning about rainforests. There wasn't any actual rain in our room, but it did look forest-ish.

She'd taped a lot of long strips of green and brown crepe paper up to dangle from the ceiling. Kids were tilting their heads back to blow at them. She'd also hooked two ropes across the room. That's where she hung our rainforest projects. It was stuff we'd made the week before in art class. There were purple paper orchid flowers and striped snakes and fruit bats with google eyes pasted on them. The new kid hadn't come yet when we made them, so she didn't get it. She shut her eyes, opened them again, and blinked.

On top of the bookcase, Mrs. Zookey had put a monkey. It was from Ben's little sister's collection of stuffed animals. The sign around its neck said RED HOWLER, but I bet it wasn't one. It was pink.

The best part of the rainforest was the long line of black plastic ants stuck on a brown rope with glue.

The ants were mine. They were supposed to be leaf-cutter ants climbing down to attack a bean plant. Patrick and me were both writing our reports on leaf-cutter ants, but since I'd brought the plastic ones to school, I got to glue them onto the rope. Mrs. Zookey had clipped it on an air vent near the door. It looked cool.

"Mr. E. made all this with magic," I whispered to Sophie. "He did it while we were eating lunch."

She was so easy to fool, I kept going. "Because of all the magic, we sometimes call our school Pigwarts." Patrick heard me and laughed.

"Richard, Patrick," Mrs. Zookey said. "Will you please stop talking and come to my desk.

"The rest of the class, use this time to continue your reports on plants and animals of the rainforest. I want each report to be interesting to read. I want it to make sense. Watch your spelling. One full page. Neatness counts."

When we got to her desk, Mrs. Zookey still did not look happy. Usually she smiles. "Boys," she said, and she sighed. "Mr. Economopoulos just told me what happened in the lunchroom."

"See, Richard didn't mean it," Patrick said. "I saw it all."

Mrs. Zookey went on like he hadn't said anything. "He said he told you there would be consequences, and indeed there will. Mr. E. and I have just decided what those consequences will be."

Patrick kept on talking. "Richie has these teeth that came out just yesterday and it still hurts him a lot and besides he said he was sorry. Right, Richie?"

Maybe he was trying to help me out. I fake-smiled to show her the empty space. I also tried to look like my no-teeth spaces hurt a lot.

Mrs. Zookey nodded. "I have noticed, Richard, that you have two missing teeth. But that does not excuse your behavior. You didn't cover your mouth when you sneezed, and you ended up covering Mr. Economopoulos with—"

"With red raspberry gelatin dessert," Patrick said. "It was a huge mess and he will never, ever do that again. Right, Richie?"

"Please stop talking, Patrick," Mrs. Zookey told him. "I think you know it is not good manners to interrupt."

Patrick looked up at the ceiling.

"The important thing," Mrs. Zookey went on, "is for you to learn from what you did. Thursday morning there is to be a second- and third-grade assembly. It will be in the Gymatorium at ten o'clock. The third-grade chorus will sing.

"At that assembly, you will give a report on manners to the entire group. In your report, you will tell the other students what you have learned about how to behave properly in the lunchroom. This is Tuesday, so you will have a full day to prepare."

"Richard won't mind doing that, will you, Richie?" Patrick asked. "I bet he'll have a lot to say."

"What? Just me?" I asked her. "No fair." Patrick smiled.

"Both of you," she said. "It will be a joint report."

She looked straight at Patrick. "Mr. Economopoulos saw that your chin was also red and sticky until you wiped it on your sleeve. He did not think it was an accident."

Patrick looked at his sleeve. It was red and sticky. "Well," he said, "anyway, it wasn't me who sneezed. It was Richie. I didn't do anything. And besides, what about the new kid? She shouldn't get off just because she's new. Did you hear about what she said to us? She called us a name, a really bad name. I'm not even going to *say* it."

Sophie whispered to Dawn Marie. Dawn Marie's eyes got big. It got whispered around. When the rest of the class heard what Patrick had said, they were talking, too. They didn't stop, either, not until Mrs. Zookey flicked the light switch off and on and said, "Class! Class!"

But Dawn Marie and the new kid went right on talking.

"Dawn Marie, do you girls have something you want to share with us?" Mrs. Zookey asked.

"Uh," Dawn Marie said, "I was just telling Sophie about how you hung the rainforest." She pointed at the ceiling like Mrs. Zookey didn't know where the crepe-paper streamers were. "She's new, so she didn't see how it got there so fast. She said Richard told her—"

And that's when Mr. E. came to the door. When he opened it, the wind made my ant-rope swing right at him. The ants must have looked real, too, because Mr. E. jumped. I poked Patrick and we laughed. Patrick and me, we were in this together. It wasn't just about me sneezing Jell-O.

Mr. E. had changed into a new green Sumac School T-shirt. It was clean. There wasn't a single smudge of bat blood on it.

Sophie looked at Mr. E. and then she looked at Patrick and me. She smiled. "Abracadabra," she whispered.

Mrs. Zookey went to the door, and she and Mr. E. talked so quiet we couldn't hear them.

"How we gonna get out of this?" Patrick whispered. "I think maybe I have a two-day sore throat." He gave a fake cough. "That should do it."

When Mr. E. left, Mrs. Zookey came back to Patrick and me. "Here's the plan," she said. "Thursday the third-grade chorus is going to perform for the assembly. Your report," she told us, "will come just after the third graders' song about manners. The seed spitters will be singing their report. They wrote the words themselves."

"The Seed Spitters? They call themselves that?"

Patrick asked her. "Maybe Richie and me could get a name, too. We could be the Vampire Sneezers. How does that sound?" His throat must have stopped being sore. "I take guitar lessons. I can sing, too."

"They do *not* call themselves seed spitters. That's what they *did*," Mrs. Zookey said. "They spat seeds and pits. What you are to do is talk about how well-mannered boys and girls should behave in the lunchroom. You must give six good solid rules. And for goodness' sake, don't try to sing them."

I could tell that Patrick was about to complain again, but Mrs. Zookey went on. "Mr. Economopoulos will speak to your parents. He will explain the assignment. Right now, though, take your seats. There's work to do."

Patrick waited at Mrs. Zookey's desk.

"Parents can't come to the assembly," he said. "Please tell me they can't."

"Parents are always welcome," Mrs. Zookey told him.

He sat down next to me and put his head in his hands. "Maybe my mom will answer the phone. Maybe she won't tell my father. He would be mad," Patrick said. "I'd be in big trouble. What am I gonna do?"

— 6 —

You Did What?

"And that nice Patrick, too?" my mom asked. "Mr. Economopoulos sounded very disappointed with both of you. What were you thinking? Well, clearly you weren't thinking."

When he called my mom, all Mr. E. said was that we had to give a report on manners. He said it was because we had misbehaved in the lunchroom. He let me tell her what we'd done. I sort of told her. I tried to clean it up so it wouldn't sound so bad.

Still, no matter how I told the story, Mr. E. ended up with red sticky sneeze stuff on his shirt.

"It's only right that you should be punished," my mom went on. "Though I think what you did is far worse than bad manners. Still, giving a report seems about right. And when you stand there before the assembly, you must remember everything I've told you about being polite."

My mom likes to talk about polite stuff. She tells me a lot. But all I could remember was, if you've got to go, you don't say, "Wait for me, I've got to pee first." I did that once and my mom said it wasn't polite. She said all I need to say before I leave for the toilet is "Excuse me." Maybe that's true, but I wasn't about to say it out loud to a bunch of kids. No way. They'd laugh at me.

Wednesday morning at library time, I checked out two books on manners. Patrick wouldn't even look at them. He said if he needed stuff, he'd look online. He said when Mr. E. called, his father answered, and he was mad. Mostly his father was mad at Mr. E. for not getting the joke. He didn't tell his father about the sneeze part, because I was the one who did it. He said he told his father that parents aren't allowed at assemblies. He said for sure his father wouldn't show up. His father is a busy man.

"I'm lucky," I told Patrick. "My mom said she wouldn't be caught dead at the assembly. She said she'd be too embarrassed. She said it looked like she hadn't done a good job with me. Like *I* was her job."

I didn't tell Patrick, but Mom still cuts up my meat. Last night she said she was going to give me lessons in how to cut steak so it's bite-sized. This is good. I like steak when I can chew it.

Patrick and I were standing in the lunch line. It wasn't moving. Some kid threw up, and they had to call a custodian to bring a mop and pail.

"We better think of six good rules for tomorrow," I told Patrick. "We can't just say, 'Don't sneeze with your mouth full and always say please and thank you.'"

"Right," Patrick agreed. "That's only three."

"How about this," I said. "You and me, we can scope out the lunchroom today and see what kids are doing that's super gross. Then tomorrow we'll just say, 'Don't do that.'" Seemed like a good idea to me.

He rolled his eyes.

"Or we could write a poem," I tried.

He rolled his eyes again. "I started one," he said. "And the only rhyme for 'manners' is 'bananers.' It wasn't funny enough."

"You're right," I told him. "A poem wouldn't work. And remember, we've got to be serious. We don't want all those kids laughing at us."

Ben and Aiden were in line, too. So were Dawn Marie and the new kid. They were talking about kickball. None of them had to figure out how to say stuff in front of the whole second and third grade. That had to be a hundred kids.

"There's something I want to ask you," Dawn Marie said to us. "I asked Sophie already. I was scared to ask the whole class about it. Some kids might think my mom is, you know, weird. Do you promise, cross your heart, not to tell?" Everybody but Patrick nodded yes and crossed their heart.

"Patrick!" Dawn Marie called. Patrick gave a big sigh and crossed his heart, too.

"Well, the thing is, my birthday party is this Saturday, and everybody in the class is invited."

"I already got an invitation in the mail," Patrick said. "So?"

Dawn Marie began to whisper. We had to lean in. "Well, my mom thought that besides the chocolate cake, she'd put out some banana bread she'd made with—instead of nuts—a bunch of cicadas.

She thought kids would like that. What do you think?"

"I think those are bugs," Aiden said.

"It's your birthday and she wants to feed us *insects?*" Patrick asked. "Your mother *is* weird."

"Is not," Dawn Marie said. "You remember cicadas. There were lots and lots of them and they were loud. My mom cut out all these pages of cicada recipes from the newspaper. And she even bought a sack of frozen ones. I had one in a cookie. It was crunchy. But if you think it's a dumb idea," she went on, "I can always tell her no."

"Tell her no!" Aiden said.

"I say, *Oui!*" Sophie shouted.

"Easy for you," I told her. "You eat snails."

"My mom says cicadas have lots of protein," Dawn Marie said.

"Ha!" Patrick said. "Protein! You want protein? I'll show you protein." He unzipped his lunchbox, reached in, and took out a plastic bowl with a lid on it. Inside was a hard-boiled egg. It was peeled.

He took the egg out of its bowl and handed the bowl to me. He held the egg up like he was a magician. "Watch this!" he said. "I bet this extra-large egg has more protein than a hundred cicadas. And you know what I'm gonna do? I'm gonna turn it into a boy. Abracadabra!" He opened his mouth super wide. Then he tossed the egg up and caught it, just like that, between his teeth.

The egg, the whole entire extra-large egg, was in Patrick's mouth. It was super big, too big to swallow.

He was showing off. I knew how to get him. Patrick got me all the time. It was my turn.

First I shut the egg bowl and gave it to him. He had the lunchbox in his other hand, so his hands were full. Then I looked behind him. Nobody was there.

So I said to nobody, "Oh, hi, Mr. E., we were just talking about eating protein — weren't we, Patrick?"

Patrick's eyes got big. He did not turn around. His cheeks were fat. He had an egg in his mouth.

The rest of the kids got it. "Hi, Mr. E.," they said.

"Patrick told us eggs have a lot of protein," Dawn Marie said to nobody.

"I heard somebody threw up," Ben said, looking up at nobody. "I bet that stinks."

I yawned. Huge. I did not cover my mouth. Mr. E. didn't care. Mr. E. wasn't there. "Oh, Mr. E.," I said, "I stayed up really late last night working on my 'Good Manners' report. I am soooo sleepy." I yawned again, bigger.

The thing about a yawn is, it's like a cold. It's catching. When you see a big yawn, you have to yawn, too.

"Stop, stop," Ben said. "Now you're making me do it," and he did.

"Oh, Mr. E.," said Dawn Marie, "you better go or you'll want to take a nap right here in the middle of the hall." She opened her mouth wide.

So did Patrick. He couldn't help it. He yawned. His hands were full with the covered bowl and the lunchbox, so he couldn't catch the egg. It oozed past his teeth and out of his open mouth. It dropped *splat* onto the hall floor. He'd squashed the egg in his mouth, so it didn't roll far. The glob of yellow and white just sat there. Patrick didn't want Mr. E. to see the egg, so he picked up his foot and he smashed it flat. He never got to turn it into a boy.

"*Au revoir,* Mr. Economopoulos. Goodbye," Sophie called. But when Patrick snapped his head around, Mr. E. was nowhere in sight.

"Wow, Patrick," Ben said. "You are one lucky duck. If Mr. E. had caught you with a whole egg stuffed in your mouth, he'd have thought you didn't know anything at all about manners. That was disgusting. I mean, a whole egg! That was huge. Was it a duck egg or something? Good thing our yawning made Mr. E. go away."

Sophie picked up the plastic bowl and lid. Ben rescued the open lunchbox and gave it to Patrick.

I scooped up most of his squashed egg. The joke was worth it. I yawned.

Patrick zipped his lunchbox shut just as the line began to move again.

He checked the hall for Mr. E. "You're right," he said. "That was close." He wiped his hands on his pants.

"Unless he *did* see it," Ben said. "He's very tall."

— 7 —
Other People's Plates

Once we made it to the lunchroom, I looked around for stuff that was bad manners. Nobody was throwing whipped-cream pies like they do in cartoons. Actually, nobody ever does that, so I could cross "food fight" off my list of things not to do.

Patrick sat down with his lunchbox. Most days I bring my Spider-Man one, but not this time. My mom said she was out of food I didn't have to bite. I stood in line and bought the soup of the day, milk, and lemon pudding. I could eat them all, easy.

Ben and Aiden sat at the same table as Patrick

and me. So did the new kid and Dawn Marie. Aiden sniffed at my soup. "They call that sweet potato and black bean chili, but it has green stuff in it. I would never eat that," he said. "Yuck! What *is* that green stuff?"

He looked like he was going to poke his finger in my soup, so I grabbed it away. "I bet it's either spinach or kale," he went on. "I hate that stuff. I brought my lunch. It's all good. I've got a PB and J, without the PB because you can't bring PB to school. I have a sack of chips and a bag of chocolate-covered raisins. I know because I packed it myself."

"To me the soup looks good," Sophie told me. "Tomorrow I will buy. Today I bring my lunch. I have the *pain* and the *jambon*."

I didn't ask if she was doing idioms again. It looked like she was eating a ham sandwich. I also didn't ask if it was true she ate snails. I was afraid she'd say yes and I'd have to say "Yuck."

The soup was so good my mom could have made it, and I was hungry. I was eating it fast. I'd stopped missing my two front teeth.

Patrick grabbed my arm. "Okay, Richie," he said. "You got paper? Write this down. Rule number one. Don't slurp your soup. I bet that's in all those books you got. Slurping soup is bad.

"What's it taste like, anyway?" he went. He pulled the spoon out of his Fruit on the Bottom blueberry yogurt and scooped some soup out of my bowl.

"Hey, cut it out!" I told him.

"Weird," he said. "It tastes like blueberry yogurt."

Ben leaned over to us and said, "Rule number two, Patrick. Don't eat off other people's plates. *A,* it's against school rules because of allergies, and *B,* Richard might get what you've got."

"No, no, it's okay," Patrick told him. "My father and me, we do it all the time." He tilted up his cup of yogurt and tapped the bottom, and what was left fell into his mouth. "You got any *good* ideas?" he asked Ben.

"My idea is that Ben and I are going to sit somewhere else," Aiden said, and they both stood up.

Dawn Marie got up, too. "See you?" she asked Sophie.

"I'm okay, thank you," Sophie said, and she waved. "'Okay' is right to say?" she asked me.

"Perfect," I told her.

"Why'd everybody go so fast?" Patrick asked.

I stayed put. We had a report to do. Sophie peeled her banana. "You do not see why they leave?" she asked Patrick. "I do. It is as big as a house to me." She took a bite of banana.

"My mother would say it's as plain as the nose on your face," I told her, and she nodded.

"Listen, what if I treat my part like a talk show?" Patrick said. "Second *and* third grades, that's a lot of fans. I wish I could play my guitar. When I told my dad this report was about eating right, you know what he said? He said you always know you're *not* eating right if you've got a pickle in one ear and a banana in the other. Get it?"

"No," Sophie said. "I do not." I shrugged. I got it, but I decided to keep her company.

"You are both dumb-heads," Patrick said. "You're about as sharp as marbles. Okay, Richie, we've gotta do three rules each. You do what you want to and I'll do my thing. I get dibs on 'Don't Sneeze with

Your Mouth Full' because I saw you do it. I'll do the 'Magic Words' one, too, about please and thank you. It'd be cheating to make that two rules, so I'll do another one I've been thinking about. It's one you'd never do, I promise. Okay?"

It was okay with me. I just wanted it to be over.

He stuffed the last of his turkey and tomato sandwich into his mouth and kept on chewing and talking. You could see mushed-up tomato and mustard and turkey between his teeth. "It doesn't matter what you say," he went on. "Nobody cares how you eat, anyway. Nobody but Mr. E."

He left his trash on the table and ran outside to the playground.

Mr. E. wandered past, looking for trouble. Sophie gathered up Patrick's leftovers. Then she nodded to Mr. E. with a serious face.

"You want to go out and play foursquare?" I asked her.

She looked at me weird, like I'd asked her if she wanted to go out and jump over houses.

"It's a game. I'll show you how," I said.

She picked up her brown bag and banana peel and tossed them and Patrick's trash into the big trash container. Then she turned to me. "'Dumbhead'?" she asked. "Is this not the same thing as 'stupid'?"

— 8 —

The Lunchroom Is No Place for That

On Thursday morning before class started, Patrick announced that he was ready to go. "I practiced," he said. "I'm good at this."

I was kind of ready, but my hands were shaking.

Mrs. Zookey heard us talking. "You boys will do just fine," she said. "The assembly starts at ten o'clock. Mr. E. will introduce you. The two of you will have ten minutes to tell the group what you know about good lunchroom manners. That shouldn't be too hard. And this is serious. No funny stuff," she told Patrick.

He shook his head.

"Do you have your reports written down?" she asked.

I showed her my two pages. It looked short. When I held it up, my report shook, too.

"I think Richard's got butterflies in his stomach," Dawn Marie told Sophie.

"Flies made of butter?" Sophie asked.

"Bigger than a fly," Dawn Marie told her, flapping her arms like wings, "and not made out of butter. It's a big flying bug."

"A bug in your stomach? You eat a bug?" Sophie asked me, like that was a really interesting thing to do.

"'Butterflies in your stomach' just means you're scared," I told her. "And I am. A little. All those kids looking at me."

"I'm not scared at all," Patrick said, but I bet he had butterflies, too.

"Wings in the stomach. I like the idiom," Sophie said. "It turns words into something else. It is magic."

The bell rang and we stood up for the Pledge of Allegiance. Ben was Mrs. Zookey's Teacher's Pet for the day. Kids like to be Teacher's Pet. You get to do good stuff. First he got to lead the Pledge. Sophie got a lot of the words wrong. Then he got to take lunch count. There was chicken noodle soup. I raised my hand for it.

Next was what Mrs. Zookey calls Yummies. Kids tell about good things like learning to dive without making a belly flop. You could also tell a Yucky, a bad thing like skinning your elbow. Dawn Marie had a Yummy. It was the chocolate cake her mom was making for her birthday party. She didn't say anything about cicadas in banana bread.

My Yucky was that I had to say two pages of manners stuff to the second and third graders and I was scared. I didn't raise my hand, though. My butterflies might not like it.

At five minutes to ten, Mrs. Zookey led us down to the big room the teachers call the Gymatorium because it's got a stage. The kids just call it the gym. The third graders were already there, sitting on the floor crisscross applesauce.

At ten o'clock on the nose, all the third graders stood up and the music teacher, Mrs. Mortimer, rapped her stick on the music stand. They sang "This Land Is Your Land," some song about miles and miles of smiles, and a few I didn't listen to, and finally they ended with "She'll Be Comin' 'Round the Mountain." They threw their arms in the air whenever they sang it. The second graders clapped like crazy.

Then the ten kids who'd been caught spitting seeds and pits climbed the steps up to the stage.

Mr. E. stood on the stage, too. Even without a microphone, his voice boomed. He said, "As you all know, this is Mind Your Manners Month at Sumac School. I hope you know that good manners are important all year round. They show our respect for other people. These third graders are going to sing a song they wrote themselves about good manners in the lunchroom."

The third graders onstage looked at each other like they weren't sure when to begin. One kid poked the guy next to him. That guy started to sing, and then the rest did, too.

They kind of swayed from side to side and went, "The more we eat together, together, together, the more we eat together, the neater we'll be. We'll chew with our mouths shut, we'll do all the nice stuff. The more we eat together, the neater we'll be."

And like that. They did five verses. In one of the verses they rhymed "food" with "good." A few kids giggled and groaned. When they were finished, the seed spitters and pit blowers bowed. The other third graders clapped like crazy. The second graders did, too.

One kid stepped forward. I heard he was the kid who brought the watermelon to school. I bet he was the chief seed spitter, too. Mr. E. must have thought so, because he was the kid who had to give a talk all by himself.

"Uh, I'm Evan," he said. "I just want to say, I mean, about watermelon seeds, there's only one time it's okay to spit them straight out. That's when you're outside and on the grass and like that and there's a contest to see who can spit them the farthest. I mean, the lunchroom is no place for that. In the lunch-room, what you do is, you put watermelon seeds and cherry pits, too, in a paper napkin. Then you put the napkin in the trash. When third graders do stuff like that, we are good role models to you second graders. Thank you for listening."

The third graders clapped again, the second graders not so much. We thought our manners were every bit as good as theirs. Maybe better. We didn't spit seeds.

Patrick and I were next. My butterflies started flapping their wings even faster, like if I threw up, they could escape.

"Thank you for your efforts, third graders," Mr. E. said.

I hoped he'd do a magic trick next. It could be about good manners. He could have whipped a big red napkin out of thin air or he might've found ten little rainbow ones in his sleeve, but he didn't. He kept on talking. "Now, two of our second graders, Richard and Patrick, want to share their thoughts on how to behave well in the lunchroom." He didn't say how I'd sprayed his shirt with bat blood. That was good, at least.

Patrick gave me a high-five.

As we climbed up the steps to the stage, some second graders started clapping. Ben did. So did Dawn Marie and Sophie. I almost felt okay.

— 9 —

I'm Not Late, Am I?

I was going first. The table and chair I needed for my talk were already on the stage. I pushed them forward and took a deep breath. I was just about to start talking when I heard this funny voice. I looked up. When Patrick heard it, he put his arms over his head and hid behind the stage curtain.

It was a high, squeaky, grown-up voice. It was a voice I'd heard before. It was the voice of Patrick's father, Mr. Olimpia. He was standing just inside the gym door. "Is this where the assembly is gonna be?" he asked. He was loud. "Is this where my kid is gonna perform? I'm not late, am I?"

Mrs. Zookey was sitting on a folding chair near the stage. She jumped up and headed to the gym door.

"Tell me the truth, now, it's okay that I'm here, right?" he asked her. "I'm big on tellin' the truth, sayin' it like it is."

"Parents are always welcome," she told him. She shook his hand. "I'm Mrs. Zookey, his teacher."

"Oh, I know you. Met you at the open house. I spoke up. I bet you remember me. I wore this same Yankees jacket."

She nodded, then she whispered in his ear and led him back to her chair.

He did not sit down. "Listen, I'm wondering," he went on in his loud voice, "what did these boys do that was so bad? You know, they're just a couple of scamps trying to get a laugh."

Mrs. Zookey held her finger to her lips and went, "Shhhhh."

He laughed and clamped his hands over his mouth. Mr. E. walked over to join them.

The kids all started talking. I could hear them asking who that guy was in the Yankees jacket. Mr. E. heard them, too. He raised his arm up high. That means stop talking. The whole room got quiet. He turned and pointed to the stage.

Everybody looked. Everybody looked at me. Patrick was still behind the curtain.

My knees felt like noodles, so I sat down in the chair. On the table I had a bowl, a spoon, and a little can of tomato juice. But that was for later.

Mrs. Zookey nodded at me and smiled like everything was just fine. I cleared my throat. She had told me to talk loud because the microphone wasn't working, so I did.

"Good manners are important," I read from my notes. "I will tell you three rules to follow in the lunchroom. Rule number one: Wash your hands before you eat. A lot of germs stick to your hands. You can't see them, but they're there. They can make you so sick you have to go to the emergency room at the hospital. Also, use the wipes on the lunchroom tables. This is good manners because giving some-body a disease is bad manners."

I looked up. So far, so good. I took a deep breath.

"I know this kid," I heard Patrick's father say. "He lives across the street from me. But just you wait till you get a load of *my* kid."

I looked at Patrick standing behind the curtain. He must have heard, too.

"Rule number two," I went on, loud and fast. I figured the faster I talked, the sooner I'd be done. "If you do something bad or gross"—and I looked over at Mr. E.—"you're supposed to say you're sorry right away and stop doing that thing. Bad stuff could be eating off somebody else's plate or chewing with your mouth open. Also, you shouldn't try to see how many soup noodles you can stuff in your mouth without swallowing or having any of them fall out."

Patrick's father was slapping his knee and

chuckling. Maybe he'd never seen noodle stuffing. Patrick does it at school. It's gross. Mrs. Zookey was not laughing. Neither was Mr. E.

I took another deep breath. I had to keep going. The last rule was the hardest. It was my mom's idea. "Showing is better than telling," she said. She thought it was such a good idea, she made me call Patrick so he wouldn't do it, too. He wasn't there, so his father took the message.

"The third rule is about soup," I read. "Almost every day the lunchroom has soup. There is a right way to eat it and there is a wrong way. Part of this rule is, don't slurp your soup." Kids laughed. Maybe "slurp" is a funny word.

I pulled the tab off the little tomato juice can and poured all the juice into the bowl. It was hard to read my report and show how to eat the soup at the same time, so I stopped reading.

"One of the manners books says you're not

supposed to fill your spoon any more than"—I checked my report—"seventy-five percent full. I don't know how much that is, but maybe *this* much." I scooped some up. "And also, you don't put the whole spoon in your mouth."

More kids laughed. "I mean the *spoon* part of the spoon," I told them. "I will show you how to do it."

"Wait, wait," I heard Patrick's father tell Mrs. Zookey. "There's a killer punch line."

Did I have a punch line? I started talking faster. "You're supposed to sip soup," I said, and I sipped some tomato juice. It wasn't too hot and it wasn't too cold. It also wasn't just right, so I made a face, like "Blech!" Was that a killer punch line?

Kids might have laughed, but Patrick came on the stage with me. He wasn't supposed to do that. He was supposed to wait behind the curtain till I was finished. When he stepped out, his father clapped. No one else did.

Patrick was breathing down my neck. I turned and told him to cut it out.

I was about to say my very last soup part, the part about not banging your spoon on the bottom of the bowl, when I looked down. I couldn't believe my eyes. I yelped. I stood up. I spilled the spoon of tomato juice.

A big black ant was floating in the middle of my bowl!

"Patrick!" I yelled. "What's that ant doing in my soup?" It was one of my plastic ants. Patrick took it off the rope and put it there! Nobody else could have.

"But wait, there's more," Patrick's father went in that high, squeaky voice.

"What's that ant doing in Richard's soup?" Patrick asked. He looked out at his father and said, extra loud, "It's doing the *backstroke*."

The kids laughed. They laughed their heads off. And Patrick's father almost doubled over, he was laughing so hard.

When he straightened up, he shouted out, "Don't tell them that! Then *everybody* will want one."

I was just standing there. Everybody was laughing at me. Patrick and his father had both made me look dumb. I felt these big, fat tears in my eyes. I wiped them away with my fists so nobody could see.

Mr. E. put his arm in the air, but nobody got quiet.

"Patrick!" Mrs. Zookey's voice sounded big and mad. "Did you just drop something into Richard's bowl of soup?"

He couldn't say no.

"It was just a joke, Mrs. Zookey," Patrick said. "We're trying to make good manners fun." He turned to Mr. E. "It was kind of like a magic trick," he told him. "I knew Richard wouldn't eat it. Besides, it's part of our report. Richard knew about it all the time."

"No way!" I shouted.

The kids laughed like I'd said something super funny. Mr. E. held his arm up again and waved it back and forth until they stopped. Mostly.

Mrs. Zookey could see how things had gone wrong. She smiled at me to make me feel better.

Then she stepped forward. "I think Richard's given us three good, useful rules," she said. "Let's give him a big Power Clap!" She used her loudest teacher voice. A Power Clap is one big clap. It's

what we always do at the end of reports. Everybody clapped. Once. All together. They clapped, but they were still laughing. At me.

— 10 —

They Eat What?

I climbed down the steps. Up on the stage, Patrick was waving, like the Power Clap was for him. "You can clean up later," he called to me. "It's my turn now." The ant trick was mean. And I'd thought we were a team.

When I got off the stage, I sat right down in the front row next to Ben and the Table Two girls. "He really got you this time," Ben said.

Patrick kept waving.

"That's my boy," Patrick's father told Mrs. Zookey. "Always on the ball." Mrs. Zookey put her finger to her lips. This time she frowned when she went, "Shhhhh."

"Welcome to 'Good Manners Can Be Fun,' part two," Patrick said in a big voice. He wasn't reading. His hands were shaking, though. He knew he got away with the joke just because his father was there.

The kids were listening hard. They didn't expect this to be funny.

"Rule number four," Patrick said, "is to always cover your mouth if you have to sneeze, especially if your mouth is already full of a whole lot of stuff, like, say, Jell-O." He grinned. "That one's for you, Richie."

Nobody laughed. Most kids hadn't heard about my Mosquito sneeze. Nobody else had seen it but Sophie.

Mr. E. didn't crack a smile.

Patrick's voice got louder. "Rule number five: Always remember to use the magic words. You know them. What are they? Everybody?"

We learned the magic words in kindergarten. A lot of kids said them with him. "Please," they said, and then "Thank you."

"Okay," Patrick told them, "that was really lame. Say them again louder." They said the words again, louder. *"Please"* and *"Thank you!"*

"I've got a rule number six, but it's more like a question. I'll tell you the rule later, okay? It's about ants. Real ones, not fake ants." He pointed at me, like I was a fake ant.

"Get this," Patrick's father said to Mrs. Zookey. "It's so creative."

Mr. E. was pacing up and down in the back of the gym. You could tell he didn't like what was happening. He didn't like it at all.

Patrick fished the ant out of my bowl with his fingers and held it up. It dripped tomato juice.

"I caught it doing the crawl," Patrick said, and kids giggled.

"Me and Richie are both doing our rain-forest reports on leaf-cutter ants," Patrick told everybody. "They are even bigger than this." He held my ant up high. "People *eat* them. The queen leaf-cutters are the tastiest. This is a true fact."

"You tell 'em, son!" his father called out. "They *egg*-specially like the queen ant's eggs."

Patrick looked out at his father. "I — I was gonna say that next," he told him. "And — and, besides," he said, "Mrs. Zookey told us that interrupting people isn't good manners."

Mr. E. stopped pacing and called out a question. "Excuse me, Patrick," he boomed, "but this seems to be a different report. What do rainforest ants have to do with lunchroom manners?" His face was red. You could tell that he was really mad.

Patrick's father leaned toward Mrs. Zookey. "I don't get it," he said. "I thought this was supposed to be a fun-filled report. I helped him out some, you know—"

He would have said more, too, but Mr. E. walked toward him with his arm raised up high for silence.

Patrick turned his back to us and crossed his arms tight.

His father looked first at Patrick and then at me. I was rubbing my eyes.

"Is this my bad?" he asked Mr. E. "My jokes are funny. They make you laugh."

Patrick turned back around. He still had his arms crossed and his mouth shut. He had stopped giving the report.

"Please answer the question, Patrick," Mrs.

Zookey said. "Is there some kind of link between ants and good manners?"

"Well," Patrick went on. He looked at his father, like now maybe he wanted some help. His father was looking at me.

I wasn't crying, no kidding. I was just sniffing up snot. It kept dripping from my nose.

Patrick sighed. "Okay," he said. "I read about

these different ants that people eat—except of course for red ants, which aren't good for you, so you shouldn't eat them. I don't know for sure, but I think eating red ants could kill you dead." Kids started going *"Eeewwwwww!"* You could tell that made Patrick happier. His audience still liked him. He smiled and kept on talking. "A lot of the ants that people eat look like Richie's ant, except they aren't plastic." They even thought *that* was funny.

He grinned big at his father and got a weak grin back.

His father shook his head and turned to Mr. E. "They're laughing at the jokes, but something's gone wrong here. I don't get it," he told Mr. E. "Do you?"

I watched to see if Mr. E. would explode. Instead he smiled. "I've got an idea," he said. Then, without even saying "Excuse me," Mr. E. left the gym in a hurry.

Mrs. Zookey wasn't going to let Patrick off the

hook. "But," she said to him, "as you well know, they don't serve ants in the school lunchroom."

Patrick dropped the big plastic ant back in my soup bowl. "But if they *did*," he said, "my father and me, we wondered, would it be okay to use your hands to pick them up? I looked, but I couldn't find any rules."

"And who do you think would be eating these ants in the school lunchroom?" Mrs. Zookey asked him.

"I don't know exactly," Patrick said, "but people from different places eat different stuff. Like snails."

His father wasn't saying anything. Patrick didn't know what to do next. Mrs. Zookey could have stopped him from talking, but she didn't. I think she was waiting for Mr. E. to come back.

"Truth," Patrick went on, "I never ate an ant." He looked out at the kids in the assembly. "Has anybody here had one?"

Mrs. Zookey looked toward the door just as Mr. E. came back in. He'd put on a jacket, and he was carrying something under his arm.

She smiled and answered Patrick.

"Yes. I ate a few once. They'd been dipped in dark chocolate." And she went on, "They were like candy. I picked them up with my fingers.

"Listen, millions of people eat insects every day. Sometimes it's because they like the taste. Sometimes it's because that's all they have to eat. Insects are served in lots of different ways in many different places.

"But I've never, ever seen any on the Sumac School menu. That means we don't need to worry about whether to use fingers or forks with ants in the lunchroom.

"So, Patrick, I want you to choose another good-manners rule and write a one-page report on it for me. Have it on my desk tomorrow. I'm sure you'll do a fine job. Thank you." Then she raised her voice. "Let's hear a big Power Clap for Patrick."

Most kids clapped. Once.

Patrick clapped with them. Then he unfolded a paper sign that was almost as big as he was. It said THE END. You could tell he'd spent a lot of time making it. There were cut-out pictures of soup and Jell-O pasted on it. Around the edges he'd drawn a parade of big black ants.

Mrs. Zookey waved at the other teachers. They were sitting on folding chairs in the back of the gym.

"Five minutes more," she told them, holding up five fingers.

My nose was still dripping. I wiped it on my shirt. It was the only snot stopper I had. Nobody saw it, but this was still bad manners.

Mr. E. grabbed Mr. Olimpia's arm and led him up the stairs to the stage.

"Second and third graders, I want you to meet Patrick's father, Mr. Olimpia. He's our visitor today." He put his arm around Patrick's father's shoulders. This was weird because I could tell, just from seeing him raise his arm and pace up and down, that he didn't like the way Mr. Olimpia had talked out.

"Our thanks to Mr. Olimpia for coming this morning," Mr. E. said. "Anybody here learn something about good lunchroom manners today? Raise your hands." Most kids did.

"I expect Patrick's father has learned something, too," Mr. E. went on. Mr. O.'s face turned bright red.

He raised his hand like the kids had done to show that it was true.

"I'm going to make a short presentation here. But I'll need an assistant, someone to help me out," Mr. E. went on. "Sophie?"

Sophie was sitting in the front row. She looked around her to see if maybe he meant someone else. When he called her name again, she climbed up the steps to the stage.

"Some of you may not have met Sophie Simeon," he said. "She joined us at Sumac School on Monday. She's from France. Sophie, I'd like you to lend me a hand."

Sophie didn't get it. She held out her hand. Mr. E. smiled and waved his arm around and around. Out of his sleeve popped a shiny black wand. He put it in Sophie's open hand.

The kids all clapped and screamed. Mr. E. was doing a magic trick!

What happened next I didn't believe then and I still don't believe now, but I saw it with my own two eyes. Mr. E. asked Sophie if she knew any magic words. "Yes, sir," she told him, "I know four." And she said them: "Please, thank you, and abracadabra."

"Very magical, indeed," Mr. E. told her. "Now, take the wand, touch Mr. Olimpia's jacket, and say each of those magic words two more times. You understand?"

Mr. Olimpia grinned. He held out his arms, like he was about to fly.

Sophie got it. She twirled the wand in a big figure eight, and then she lightly touched the jacket. The gym was totally quiet. The first two magic words she whispered slow. She did that two times. And then when she shouted, "Abracadabra! Abracadabra!" Mr. E. waved his fingers like snakes and reached down the back of Mr. Olimpia's jacket. You can't guess what he pulled out.

It was a brand-new green Sumac School T-shirt, size XXXXL.

Sophie squealed. The kids yelled.

Mr. E. held the shirt up so everyone could see. Then he presented it to Patrick's father.

Mr. Olimpia totally broke up. I never saw anybody laugh that hard. First he held the T-shirt up. Then he took off his Yankees jacket and put the shirt on. He was about as tall as Mrs. Zookey, so he was little and the shirt was big. It hung all the way down to his knees.

The kids were all standing up. They clapped their hands and they stamped their feet on the gym floor.

"The joke's on me," Mr. Olimpia said. "I'm wearing it."

He waved to Patrick, and then he and Mr. E. walked down the stage steps and into the hall. The green Sumac School T-shirt, size XXXXL, flapped as he walked.

The third graders filed out, and the second graders followed.

As they walked, the third graders were singing,
"The more we eat together, together, together . . ."

My butterflies were gone.

— 11 —

My Turn

Back in our room, I tried to wipe the tomato juice off my shirt, but it was already dry. Sophie raised her hand. Mrs. Zookey called on her.

"You forget me. I have the good manners report, too," Sophie said. "Is it my turn, please?"

"No, Sophie," Mrs. Zookey spoke slowly, "you did not understand. The report was for Richard and Patrick. It was meant to help them learn how to eat their food in a nicer way."

"But I have the report, too," Sophie went on. "Mr. E. says there are consequences. It is a hard word

to spell, but I look it up. Please, I do my consequences, too." She stood up at Table Two. In front of
her was a small brown paper bag. "Thank you," she
said. "And please, also."

Mrs. Zookey let her do it. Sophie was new. Also,
she said the magic words.

"Five minutes only," Mrs. Zookey said. She sat
down on her big blue exercise ball. She told Sophie
to begin.

Sophie opened the paper bag. She took out a plastic cup. It had wobbly red stuff in it. I didn't have to ask what the red stuff was. I knew. So did Patrick.

"I will show you what I learn," Sophie said to the class. "It is how to eat this. You do not use the spoon." She pulled one out of the bag, held it up, and then dropped it back inside. "No," she said, "you eat by suction. Dawn Marie, she tells me this word."

Dawn Marie smiled like she was proud.

Sophie reached back in the bag and pulled out a straw. She held it up for everyone to see. "This is the sucker," she said. "If you use it wrong, it makes bad manners."

Patrick and I both sucked in our breath and held it. Was she really going to do what we thought she was going to do?

"First you put the sucker—" she began.

"Straw," Mrs. Zookey told her. "We call it a straw."

"First you put the . . . straw in the jelly. Then you straw in —"

"Suck in," Mrs. Zookey said.

We all watched and listened while Sophie sucked in . . . really hard. She sucked in over and over until her cheeks puffed out. Her mouth was full of oozy red Jell-O. The straw was still in her mouth. She pointed it at Patrick and me. I closed my eyes.

Patrick couldn't take it. "Don't do it!" he called. He was not cool.

I opened my eyes. It was like Sophie had sucked all the sound out of the room. She was standing in front of the class with her mouth full of vampire-bat blood.

Just when I thought she couldn't hold it any longer, she took the straw out of her mouth and swallowed. Then she burped. Big. *"Urp!"* When she did it, she held her hand over her mouth. "Pardon me," she said.

"I know good manners," she told Mrs. Zookey. "I know to cover up my mouth when I make the burp.

"I make the big one like it is good manners to do in China. Patrick, he teaches me that."

Patrick groaned.

"Good manners," she went on, "is when you keep the jelly in your mouth. You suck in," she said. "You do not blow out.

"This is an okay way to eat the jelly, no?" she asked Mrs. Zookey.

Mrs. Zookey stood up, and her exercise ball rolled back to the wall. "Well, Sophie," she said, "I don't think . . . I mean, I think . . . that it is . . ." She smiled. " . . . Unusual. I prefer the usual way, with a spoon."

A few kids laughed. I bet they'd heard about

The Mosquito. Teachers don't know about things like that.

"This way of eating," Sophie went on, "it is the same as a bug's name."

"She's going to tell about me drooling vampire blood," Patrick whispered. "I knew she was a snitch."

"I do not know what name you call this bug," Sophie said. "In France we say *papillon*."

"Mosquito," Patrick said out loud. When kids looked at him, he shrugged and said, "Well, that's what I call it."

Mrs. Zookey gave him a long look. "Butterfly," she said. "In French, a butterfly is called a *papillon*. And Sophie is quite right, the butterfly has no mouth. It eats through a long tube that is much like a straw. It's called a proboscis. The way Sophie sucked in the soft gelatin is pretty much the way a butterfly sucks in sweet nectar from flowers."

"Is this the same insect Richard had in his stomach?" Sophie asked.

It had come back. "It's still there," I told her.

Patrick put his head on his desk. He covered it with his arms.

"Sophie, just a moment," Mrs. Zookey said. "Can you tell me where you learned about the right way and the wrong way to eat like a . . . butterfly? We're talking about lunchroom manners. Did you see this in the lunchroom?"

Patrick raised his head. "I bet she's making this big pot of white cabbage in her head, right?"

Mrs. Zookey frowned. She was thinking that Sophie wasn't cooking anything. I could tell.

"No," Sophie said, "I am not."

This is it, I thought. *This time she's going to tell everything she saw in the lunchroom, and Patrick and I won't have recess for the rest of second grade. Maybe all of next year, too.*

"I am not making white cabbage," Sophie said. By now the kids and Mrs. Zookey must have thought Sophie and Patrick had gone totally bananas. She looked at Mrs. Zookey. "I am drawing a blank," she said. "Also I think the cat gets my tongue.

"That is my report," she went on. "The good manners fly of butter keeps the jelly always in its mouth. Thank you." She gave a big bow.

She sat down. There was red Jell-O on her chin.

Mrs. Zookey smiled. "Thank you, Sophie, for that fine report on good manners. We will keep it in mind. It was right on point, too." She pointed at the crepe paper hanging above her. "There are lots of *papillons* in the rainforest."

Sophie got a huge Power Clap.

"I make a good consequence?" she asked me. "It is okay? What do you think, *mon ami*?"

Mrs. Zookey was still smiling. She didn't look mad at Patrick and me. "Almost time for lunch," she said. "Gather up your belongings."

"The report was okay," I told Sophie. Everything had worked out fine. "*Mon ami*? Is that another one of those French idioms?"

"Oh, no," she told me. "Mr. E., he says the idiom does not mean what it says. These words say 'my friend,' and that is what they mean."

She was not making a joke. She meant it. I was Sophie's friend.

"Tomorrow," she told me, "I am the Teacher's Pet. Does this mean what it says?"

— 12 —

Yum

Friday morning, Mrs. Zookey let Sophie and me come into the room five minutes before the rest of the kids. Mrs. Zookey sat at her desk, grading math sheets. My job was to show Sophie what Teacher's Pet does.

She knew about Yummies and Yuckies. For her Yummy she brought treats in a big blue bowl. It was covered with shiny foil.

"My papa, he makes them this morning," she said. "I eat one already." She put the bowl on Mrs. Zookey's desk.

"I bet they're snails," I said, and moved away.

"The *escargots?*" she asked. "But no, you eat the *escargots* while they are hot and they make the sizzle in the pan. I do not bring the snails. To eat the snails with the garlic sauce, you come to Chez Paul Henri. Yes?"

I didn't say no.

"This Yummy," she said, "it is not on the menu at the restaurant of my papa."

The bell rang, and the rest of the kids came in. Patrick put his report on Mrs. Zookey's desk. It was one page long with crayon drawings. It had a long title: WHEN YOU YAWN, BE SURE TO COVER YOUR MOUTH.

When he stuck out his foot to "accidentally" trip me, I hopped right over it. He does this every day.

"I never really try to trip you," Patrick told me. "That wouldn't be right, and I always do the right thing. On the ball, that's me."

I rolled my eyes. He didn't trip me because I jumped over his foot.

Sophie stood up in front of the class, just like I'd told her to. She put her hand on her heart and led the Pledge. This was her new country, and she'd learned all the words. I gave her a little help with lunch count, and then it was time for Yummies and Yuckies.

Latille said she had a brand-new baby brother. She wasn't sure if he was a Yummy or a Yucky. Gerard told everybody he could stand on his hands for seven seconds. Mrs. Zookey let him show us. Patrick said his father wanted to turn in his new T-shirt for an XXXXS. I think that was a joke.

But what everybody wanted to do most was taste Sophie's Yummies.

"My papa, he is a chef," Sophie told us. "I tell him I need a Yummy. He buys what I ask and he cooks them crispy like *les frites,* what you call the

French fries." She whipped the foil off the top of the bowl. *"Voilà!"* she said.

It was a bowl of fried bugs.

They were mealworms.

Mrs. Zookey caught her breath. Then she smiled and took one. She looked at Patrick. "I think," she said, "that it is perfectly good manners to use your fingers when you eat mealworms." She ate the bug in two bites. "It is crunchy and tastes a little like nuts," she told us. "Would anyone else like one? You don't have to, you know. Anyone have a mealworm allergy?"

Then Dawn Marie took one. "It's okay plain," she told us, "but I'd like it better in a cookie."

A few kids came up to Mrs. Zookey's desk. They looked in the blue bowl. Some kids said "Yum" and some said "Yuck."

Mr. E. rapped on the classroom door. Mrs. Zookey waved him in.

As soon as he stepped inside the room, he raised both of his hands high. "Boys and girls," he said, "I think you've learned a great deal during this first week of Mind Your Manners Month. And I want to thank you for your cooperation and enthusiasm."

Dawn Marie was finishing off her mealworm. "Needs salt," she told Sophie, who took another one.

"My," Mr. E. said to Mrs. Zookey. "Is it time for treats so early?"

She smiled and nodded. And without looking,

he popped one into his mouth like it was a peanut. It must have felt funny on his tongue, because he leaned over to see what was in the bowl. He must have thought it was popcorn or something. He blinked. Twice. He did not chew. He did not swallow. He looked at Mrs. Zookey.

"Sophie's father, Chef Paul Henri, made them this morning," she told him. "They're mealworms. He fried them crispy like French fries."

Mr. E. still had not chewed. He still had not swallowed. He stared in the blue bowl. His eyes got big, and he clapped his hand over his mouth.

I looked at Patrick, and Patrick looked at me. We both smiled.

"We studied mealworms this year," Patrick told Mr. E. "We gave them names. One of mine was Spike. He was a good worm. I measured him with a ruler."

"I called one of mine Uncle Ken," I told Mr. E. "He turned into a beetle."

All the kids but Sophie had been in Mrs. Zookey's room when we did mealworms. They started calling out their mealworms' names, like Bubbles and Michael Jordan.

Mr. E. looked almost as green as his Sumac School T-shirt. He still had not chewed. He still had not swallowed. You could tell he wanted really bad to say something, but he couldn't talk. A little spit came out of the corner of his mouth. I hoped he wouldn't sneeze. He looked again at Mrs. Zookey.

"Mr. E.," she said. "I have a great idea. You have kept that mealworm nice and warm. Now instead of swallowing it, how about wrapping it up in this?" She reached for the tissue box on her desk, pulled out a tissue, and gave it to him.

He took it and raised it to his mouth. Before

you could say "abracadabra" twice, he had spat the soggy mealworm into the tissue.

"And that," Mrs. Zookey told us, "is exactly what you should do with something you'd rather not have in your mouth, like a watermelon seed, a cherry pit, or possibly even a mealworm." She smiled a very big smile. "That was an excellent demonstration, Mr. E."

He cradled the tissue in his hand. "Thank you, Mrs. Zookey," he said. He looked out at the class. We had not laughed. We knew better. "Happy manners to you all," he said.

When he left, the room was quiet, until Patrick said really loud, "I would never eat a mealworm. They wiggle."

"They do not wiggle," Sophie told him. "They are cooked." She picked up her third worm and put it in her mouth. She slowly chewed and swallowed it. "You see," she said to the class. "The fingers in the nose!"

We all stared at her, waiting. She did not stick her fingers in her nose.

Sophie stared back. "In English you do not say this?" she asked. "In France we say this many, many times: *Les doigts dans le nez.* It is not about fingers or noses. It only means, 'This is *very* easy to do.'"

"It's an idiom," Mrs. Zookey told the class. "It's like 'easy as pie.' When Sophie eats a mealworm, it's so easy, she could do it with her fingers in her nose."

She moved the bug bowl to the front of her desk. "I'll leave this right here," she said. "In case anyone wants to nibble."

I didn't nibble. Neither did Patrick. We didn't nibble together. We laughed instead.

"I think," Mrs. Zookey said, "we've had quite enough excitement for now. Let's do some silent reading. It's time to gather your books."

Then she leaned down between Patrick and me. "Do I need to separate you two?" she asked. "Perhaps one of you should sit at Table Six." Four quiet kids sat at Table Six.

I shook my head. Patrick said, "No way. Richie . . . I mean, Richard and I are friends. We promise not to talk too much."

She narrowed her eyes at us. Then she said,

"Fine, but I want you both to watch out for flying insects. They can get you in trouble."

When she walked away, I turned to Patrick and Patrick turned to me. "She's still gonna let us sit together," he whispered.

But Patrick and me, we had to toe the line. We had to keep our noses clean. It wouldn't be easy.

I saw this picture in my head of Patrick and me putting our toes on a line and trying to stick our fingers into our soapy clean noses. I laughed out loud. And that's when a big cartoon light bulb lit up over my head.

"Listen," I whispered to Patrick. "I just figured out an idiom." I looked over at Mrs. Zookey. She was sitting on her big blue exercise ball. "See her? She's sitting on the ball. No idiom. She's really on it, right?"

"Right," Patrick said. "I get it. The thing about

Mrs. Zookey is, no matter what happens, she knows what to do and she does it. She's on the ball. That's why . . ."

And we said it together, "Mrs. Zookey is an idiom!"

She looked up at us and put her finger to her lips. "Shhhhh."

She opened her book for silent reading.

We opened our books, too.

Patrick scribbled out a note and passed it to me. Richard, it said, I've got this great joke. My father told it to me. You're gonna laugh your head off.

And he signed it, Your friend, Patrick.